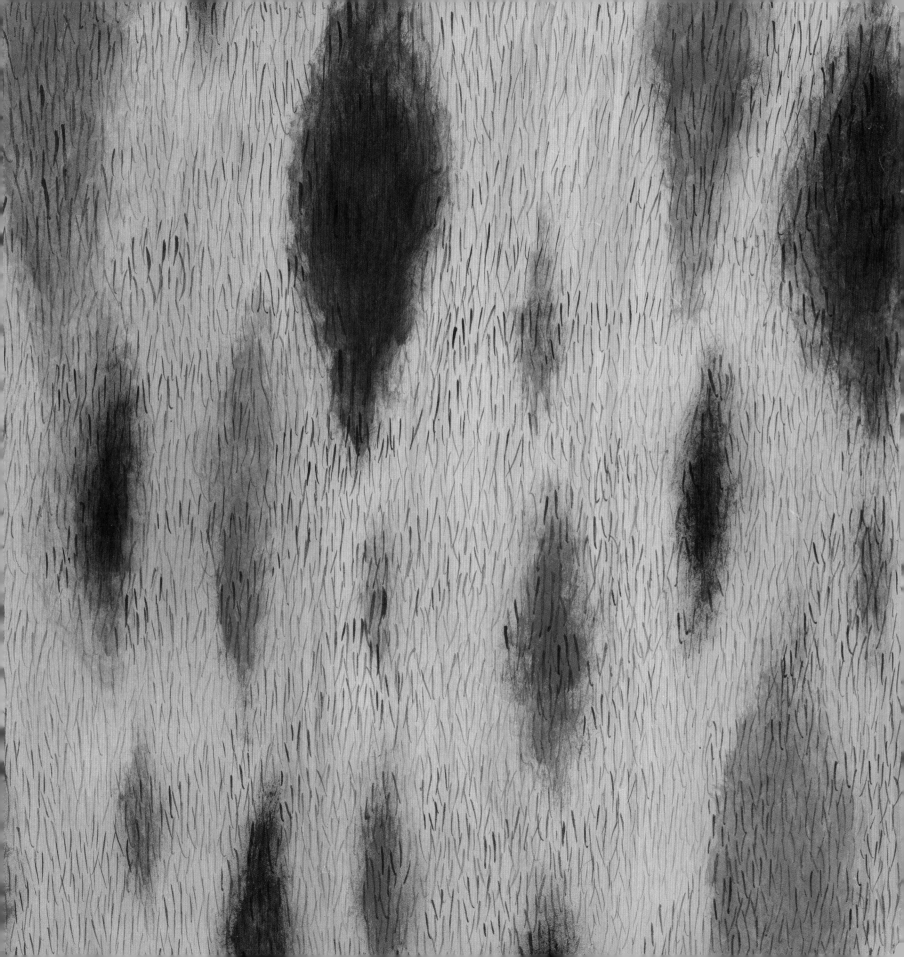

MEET WILD BOARS

MEG ROSOFF AND SOPHIE BLACKALL

SQUARE
FISH

HENRY HOLT

SQUARE
FISH

An Imprint of Macmillan

MEET WILD BOARS. Text copyright © 2005 by Meg Rosoff.
Illustrations copyright © 2005 by Sophie Blackall. All rights reserved. Printed in China. For information,
address Square Fish, 175 Fifth Avenue, New York, N.Y. 10010.

Square Fish and the Square Fish logo are trademarks of Macmillan
and are used by Henry Holt and Company under license from Macmillan.

Library of Congress Cataloging-in-Publication Data
Rosoff, Meg. Meet wild boars / Meg Rosoff and Sophie Blackall.—1st ed.
p.   cm.
Summary: It is very hard to be friends with wild boars because they are dirty and smelly, bad-tempered, and rude.
ISBN-13: 978-0-312-37963-6
ISBN-10: 0-312-37963-3
[1. Wild boar—Fiction. 2. Behavior—Fiction. 3. Humorous stories.] I. Blackall, Sophie, ill. II. Title.
PZ7.R719563Me 2005 [E]—dc22   2004008985

Originally published in the United States by Henry Holt and Company
Square Fish logo designed by Filomena Tuosto
Designed by Patrick Collins
Hand-lettering by Sophie Blackall
The artist used gouache on watercolor paper to create the illustrations for this book.
First Square Fish Edition: September 2008
10 9 8 7 6 5 4 3 2 1
www.squarefishbooks.com

For Gloria (who invented Wild Boars)
—M. R.

For Nick, the funniest man I know
—S. B.

BORIS

MORRIS

HORACE

DORIS

This is Boris.

This is Morris.

This is Horace.

This is Doris.

They are wild boars.

They are
dirty and smelly,
bad-tempered and rude.
Do you like them?

Never mind.

They do not like you either.

If you are polite to Boris and hold the door for him
he will tusk you with his horrible tusks.

TUSK TUSK TUSK.

Bad Boris.

STOMP
STOMP
STOMP

If you share your treats with Morris
he will stomp on them with his beastly feet.

STOMP STOMP STOMP.

Naughty Morris.

If you try to help Horace with his mittens
he will make a nasty smell and snort with laughter.

SNORT SNORT SNORT.

Horrid Horace.

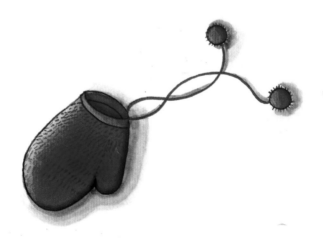

And as for Doris—

oh, my my.

She is **STINKIER** than a stinkpot turtle.

She is **UGLIER** than an Ugli fruit.

She is **BOSSIER** than a Bossysaurus.

Poor wild boars.
Nobody loves them.

Maybe just once they could come to your house.

You could make them
some snacks.

You might show them your toys,

play dress-up or dominoes...

...splash in the bath.

They could borrow pajamas
and sleep in your room.

Nice wild boars.
Sweet wild boars.
They promise
just this once
they will try to be good.

OH NO THEY WILL NOT.

Horace will soak in the toilet for hours

he'll eat all your soap

clip his toenails in bed

be rude to your pets

cut the strings off your puppets

make fun of your feet

lock himself in the shed.

Morris won't eat what you give him for supper

or let you go first

say "excuse me"

or "please."

He'll sneer and he'll scratch

stick his snout up your jumper

then eat all your chocolate

and give you his fleas.

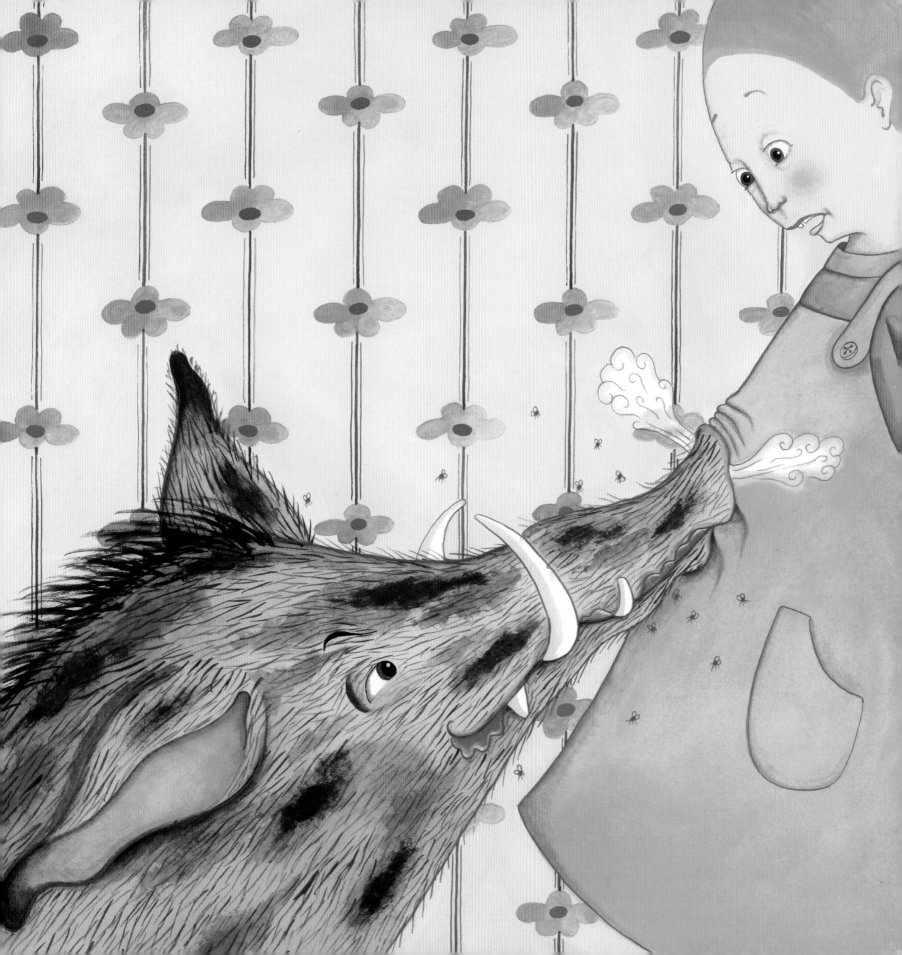

Boris will break every one of your pencils

he'll smash up your puzzles

and use all your glue

make horrible smells

leave the tops off your pens

stamp his foot

have a tantrum

then swear it was you.

And as for Doris
(who has never been good,
not for one single second—
not once
not ever
never)
she will ask for a toy in case she gets
lonely and scared in the dark.
Dear little Doris!

To which we say

HA!

Given half a chance

(or even less)

Doris will eat your very best whale,

flippers and all.

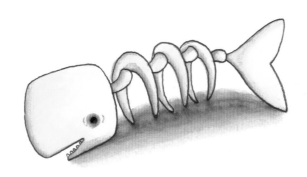

So perhaps it is best if we all agree
that there is no such thing as a nice wild boar.

Then if you happen to run across one
that is fluffy and sweet
(though chances are that you won't)
you will be very pleasantly amazed.

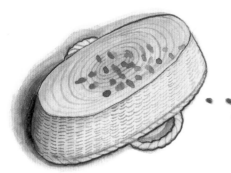

But not at all fooled.

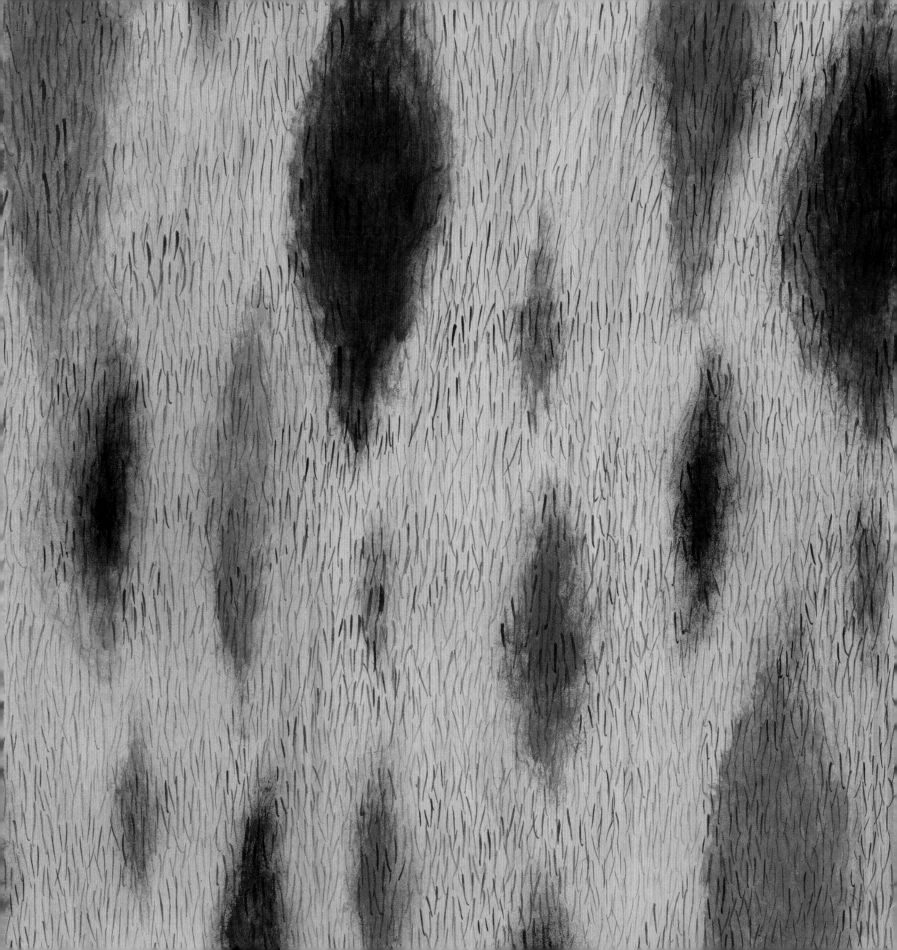